Copyright © 2010 by NordSüd Verlag AG, CH-8005 Zürich, Switzerland.
First published in Switzerland under the title *Niklas aus dem Wichtelland*.
English text copyright © 2010 by North-South Books Inc., New York 10001.
Translated by NordSüd Verlag AG. Edited by Susan Pearson. Designed by Pamela Darcy.
First published in the United States, Great Britain, Canada, Australia, and New Zealand in 2010
by North-South Books Inc., an imprint of NordSüd Verlag AG, CH-8005 Zürich, Switzerland.
Distributed in the United States by North-South Books Inc., New York 10001.
Library of Congress Cataloging-in-Publication Data is available.
Printed in Germany by Grafisches Centrum Cuno GmbH & Co. KG, 39240 Calbe, June 2010.
ISBN: 978-0-7358-2335-8 (trade edition)
1 3 5 7 9 ❋ 10 8 6 4 2
www.northsouth.com

FSC
Mixed Sources
Product group from well-managed
forests and other controlled sources

Cert no. SGS-COC-007065
www.fsc.org
©1996 Forest Stewardship Council

Advent Elf

by Päivi Stalder

Illustrated by Barbara Korthues

NorthSouth
New York / London

Paul was six when he found out he had an Advent Elf. Here's how it happened.

The whole family was in the living room—Mom, Dad, Paul's big sister, Mia, and their cat, Susie. It was the first day of Advent. Every year they had an Advent wreath, and they had lit the first candle just that evening.

Suddenly the flame flickered.

"What was that?" said Paul.

"Just a flicker," said Mom.

"Nothing to worry about," said Dad.

"Candles do that sometimes," said Mia.

They all went back to what they were doing, but
Paul just sat there, staring. And that's when he saw it.

A tiny elf was standing on the wreath tugging on a bright red scarf that was tangled in the pine needles. The little man was pulling so hard, his face was as red as his scarf. Carefully, Paul reached over and untangled it.

As quick as a wink, the elf grabbed his scarf and hopped off the table. Susie meowed, and her eyes gleamed. Paul looked under the table. The little man was running as fast as his tiny legs would carry him—under Dad's chair, behind the chest, out the door, and down the hall, straight to Paul's room. Paul raced after the elf into his bedroom and slammed the door.

The little man wasn't under Paul's bed. Or in his toy boat. Or hidden behind his stuffed elephant. There was nothing, not even a red scarf, to be seen.

Then a small voice said, "Can you *help* me?" There he was, on top of the comforter.

"I said, 'Can you *help* me?'" said the elf a little louder.

"Help you how?" Paul asked.

"Help me get home, of course," said the elf. "I'm not supposed to be here."

"Who are you?" asked Paul.

"Arty's the name," said the little man, sliding down the comforter. "Short for Artimus. I'm your Advent Elf."

"My what?" said Paul.

"Advent Elf," Arty repeated. "I'm supposed to watch over you during Advent. Keep you out of trouble. Find presents to put in your Advent calendar. That sort of thing."

"Looks like you need someone to watch over *you*," said Paul.

"I'm still in training," said Arty. "I just got started when I fell out of your wreath. I need to get back."

Before Paul could say a word, Arty leaped off the bed and dashed to the door.

"WAIT!" shouted Paul. "My cat is out there! Susie will gobble you up, just like a mouse!"

Arty stopped in his tracks and stamped his foot. "Well, how am I going to get back then?" he demanded. "This is all your fault."

"How is it *my* fault?" Paul asked.

"It's your Advent wreath, isn't it," said Arty. "So you have to get me home."

Paul sighed. How on earth was he going to get an elf back to elf land? Then suddenly he had an idea! He grabbed his *Big Book of Gnomes and Goblins* and opened it to the middle.

"You could jump in here," he suggested.

Arty snorted. "Don't be ridiculous! I'm an *elf*, not a gnome. And certainly not a goblin."

"What if I build you a paper airplane and you fly back?"
Paul suggested.

"I might just as easily sail this boat out the window,"
said Arty. "And besides, it's cold out there." He scratched
his head. "I need to get back to the Advent wreath. That's
how I got here, and that's how I'll get back."

"But, Susie . . . ," said Paul.

"I need a disguise," said Arty.

"Bear!" Paul shouted. "I could hide you in my teddy bear!"

So Arty snuggled between Bear's fuzzy arms, and
Paul carried him back to the Advent wreath. Arty
jumped off and into the wreath. The candle fizzled
and flickered and then went out.

"That's certainly a flickery candle," said Mom, looking over at the wreath.

But by then Arty was nowhere to be seen.

That night Paul's dreams were full of elves. When he woke in the morning, he wondered if he had really seen Arty at all. Had the tiny Advent elf been only a dream? Probably, he thought as he climbed out of bed.

And that's when he saw, nestled among his toys, a tiny red scarf.